The Mermaid's Gift

Claudia Cangilla McAdam • Illustrated by Traci Van Wagoner

PELICAN PUBLISHING COMPANY

GRETNA 2015

The word "Pelican" and the depiction of a pelican are trademarks of Pelican Publishing Company, Inc., and are registered in the U.S. Patent and Trademark Office.

ISBN 9781455621088
E-book ISBN 9781455621095

Printed in Malaysia

Published by Pelican Publishing Company, Inc.
1000 Burmaster Street, Gretna, Louisiana 70053

With love for my granddaughter Eleanor, whose imagination inspires me
— *C.C.M.*

Long ago on the tiny island of Burano, a young fisherman named Gianni rubbed his raw hands together and stepped into his boat. The icebound lagoon had kept the fishermen from the sea all winter. Now it was starting to thaw, but the weather still chilled the skin. Gianni pointed the bow of his boat into the wind. He rowed with the strength of ten men.

"Fool," the older fishermen hollered. "Come back! You will freeze to death!"

Gianni wouldn't turn back. His people were starving.

From the church of San Martino, Nicoletta watched his boat escape the icy grip of the shoreline. She started each day praying for her family and friends. Now, she added another whispered plea. "Protect Gianni," she begged.

For hours, Gianni lowered his nets and hauled them in again, dripping and empty. The little boat lurched and rocked, and the wind whistled up his sleeves and shoved freezing fingers down the back of his collar. With stiff, red hands, he gathered the net and flung it over the side. "One more try!"

Nicoletta sat in a small house with the other women, mending nets, tending to children, and stirring bubbling pots of thin porridge.

"Your love is a loon," one woman said. "He risks his life for what?"

Nicoletta kept her eyes on her work, but answered softly, "For you. For me. For all of us." He fished, she knew, so that they could eat, and if the catch was large, Gianni might sell much of it across the lagoon in Venice. He would buy the old stone cottage next to the church, and they could marry.

The gathering storm growled at Gianni and pelted him with icy rain. Tiny, frozen daggers of sleet lashed his face. A distant roar raced toward him, and a giant wave broke over the craft.

"No!" Gianni screamed as the breaker washed him from the boat. He somersaulted deeper and deeper into the frigid water. The powerful sea pinned him beneath the surface, his lungs burning for air, his body growing stiff with cold.

Dark clouds blanketed the island—so black it was as if night had tucked Burano into bed hours early. Nicoletta rushed outside, searching for some sign of Gianni, but she saw nothing except the inky sea.

Her sandaled feet slapped the cobbled streets as she dashed to the church and to the long rope that dangled from the bell tower. She tugged again and again, and the clanging alarm soon had the entire village rushing to the church.

"Bring lanterns and torches! Candles, too," she cried. "We'll make the bell tower a lighthouse for Gianni."

Finally, Gianni surfaced, his teeth chattering behind purple lips. His boat was nowhere to be seen. His soaked clothes weighed him down, and he could scarcely move. "Nicoletta, I'm sorry. I love you."

The beating rain died away, and in its place, magnificent music filled his ears. One glorious voice sang to him a heavenly melody with words he couldn't understand. He paddled toward the sound, and there in front of him floated one oar. Gianni clung to the wood, exhausted and frozen. He shut his eyes and rested his head against the smooth lumber.

Inside the church that smelled of candle wax and incense, Nicoletta tended the lamps in the bell tower. At last the sky lightened and the sun peeked out, painting a rainbow arch over the lagoon. "You are out there, Gianni, I know it," she said as she blew out the last flame. "Follow the rainbow home to me."

Music woke Gianni. The figure of a woman glided before him, a golden glow surrounding her. He licked salt from his cracked lips. "Are you an angel?" he asked.

She smiled and tossed her head, blonde hair swirling around her like kelp dancing in the surge of the sea. "Come with me," she sang, reaching for the oar. She swam, towing Gianni along, a sleek tail of glistening scales propelling her through the water.

She led him to his boat, still upright on the sea. Gianni dragged himself aboard. "Thank you." His voice croaked from the brine that coated his throat.

"Nicoletta waits for you," she sang. Her tail whipped the water, stirring up a froth that rose like mist above the tiny boat. It settled over Gianni in folds of delicate white lace.

"A gift for the bride," her voice rang out. "A veil for her wedding day!" With that, she vanished.

From her perch in the bell tower, Nicoletta spotted a small boat on the horizon. She skipped down the stairs and rushed through the church, pausing long enough to kneel and offer a prayer of thanksgiving.

"Gianni!" she screamed from the shoreline as the villagers gathered around. Soon, he was in her arms, cold and wet—but alive.

"I've got no fish," he said. "But I do have this." He pulled the lace from the boat and told everyone about the mermaid and her gift. "It is a wedding veil for you, Nicoletta."

"No," she answered. "We must sell it. We could feed the whole island."

An older woman stroked the lace. "I'd buy it from you, straight away, if I'd but coin to spare," she said. "I have never seen such beautiful work."

"Nor I," said Nicoletta. Her eyes brightened, and her lips parted at the wonder of an idea. "Let's use it as a guide! We can make lace just like this to sell to the princes and noblewomen of Venice." So they set to work tracing the patterns of ripples and curling waves, fan-shaped shells, and overlapping scales—like those on a mermaid's tail.

"The first piece must be an altar cloth for San Martino," Nicoletta instructed, and the others nodded in agreement. When it was finished, they made handkerchiefs and frilly collars, table linens and christening gowns. The lace was as soft as strands spun by a silkworm and as fine as a spider's web.

When all the ice melted from the lagoon, Gianni and the other fishermen loaded the merchandise into the island's largest boat and set sail for Venice. They soon returned with crates overflowing with food and with money sacks bulging with coins.

"They want more!" Gianni cried. "As much lace as can be made!"

He bought the stone cottage next to the church, and Nicoletta ran the village lace-making shop on the ground floor.

They married on the first day of May, and Nicoletta wore the lace veil that Gianni couldn't bring himself to sell. When they said their vows, a hauntingly beautiful song soared across the sea and filled the sanctuary of San Martino.

And even if all the fish swam from the lagoon, everyone on the little island knew that they would never be hungry again—thanks to the gift of the mermaid's lace.

The Mermaid's Gift weaves together fact and a fable about a mermaid to tell the tale of how the lace-making industry began on the Italian island of Burano, situated in the Venetian lagoon.

Legend has it that five hundred years ago, a fisherman from the island encountered a mermaid while out in the lagoon. She magically created a length of lace by whipping the water with her tail, fashioning the delicate fabric from the sea foam. This became the bridal veil for the fisherman's betrothed. The story goes that the other young ladies on the island loved the veil so much, they copied the pattern, and the Burano lace-making industry was born.

The more realistic origin of the industry, however, is that the women of Burano, skilled in mending their husbands' fishing nets, took up lace-making as a pastime. The lace they produced in the sixteenth century grew very popular and was exported throughout Europe. The industry began its decline, however, in the seventeenth century.

By 1872 the lace-making trade on the island had vanished, but that year a freezing winter covered the lagoon in ice, making fishing impossible. It is said that a school teacher on the island convinced an elderly lady to share the long-held secrets to making Burano lace. The teacher opened a school of lace-making, which trained hundreds of local girls and women to once again produce the lace. They stitched beauty from hardship.

A century after it began, the lace-making school closed, and in its place today, Burano maintains the Lace Museum, so that the charming craft will be preserved.

The characters in **The Mermaid's Gift** show what living a virtuous life entails, and their actions reveal the good that comes from sacrifice and perseverance. Parents and grandparents, teachers and librarians can explore and discuss with children the heroic actions of the courageous and compassionate fisherman, Gianni, and the prayerful faithfulness and creativity of loyal Nicoletta, his future wife. They are two individuals who emulate the character traits that surely must have been present in the fishermen and lace-makers of sixteenth-century Burano.

—Claudia Cangilla McAdam